Max and Moritz

Max and Moritz

WILHELM BUSCH

**Translated from the German
by Mark Ledsom**

PUSHKIN CHILDREN'S

Pushkin Press
71–75 Shelton Street
London WC2H 9JQ

English translation © 2019 Mark Ledsom

Max and Moritz was first published as *Max und Moritz* in Germany, 1865

First published by Pushkin Press in 2019

9 8 7 6 5 4 3 2 1

ISBN 13: 978-1-78269-253-9

Illustrations by Wilhelm Busch
Designed and typeset by Tetragon, London
Printed and bound by TJ International, Padstow, Cornwall

www.pushkinpress.com

Max and Moritz

*For my own (usually) much
better behaved Max—and his
"saintly" siblings, Kurt and Anya!*

Introduction

Many stories have been told
Of children who were good as gold,
But these two boys played darker games:

Max and Moritz were their names.

Instead of trying to be good
(As all young children really should),
They laughed at those who stuck to rules,
Giggling like two cackling fools:
"Playing tricks on everyone,
That's the way to make life fun!
Catching people unawares,
Stealing apples, plums and pears.
That's the way we spend our time,
With clever pranks and daring crime.
We can't see much point at all
In wasting time at church or school!"
But, oh, dear readers, it's too late
To steer them to a better fate.
You'll see the way our story ends
Is not so nice for these foul friends.
Their nasty acts, their final plight,
It's all set down in black and white.

First Prank

Of all the animals that there are,
Birds must be the best by far...
Whether chicken, duck or goose,
There's first the eggs that they produce,
And then, unlike a dog or horse,
You can cook a bird of course!
Even when no longer living,
They're the gifts that keep on giving—
Their feather bedding keeps us tight
And warm and cosy through the night.

Look, here comes old Widow Palmer,
A kind and gentle lady farmer.

In her yard, four feathered friends—
A cockerel and three well-fed hens.
Their peaceful life looks set to last,
Till Max and Moritz wander past!
Each, with evil in his head,
Reaches out and grabs some bread.

Four small morsels are soon found
Looking harmless on the ground.
But Max and Moritz, oh so rotten,
Have tied the pieces up with cotton.

Spread out cross-like on the floor,
The trap awaits our feathered four.

Sure enough, the cockerel goes
And takes a peek, then proudly crows:
"Cock-a-doodle, doodle-dee!"
The chickens follow, one, two, three...

Greedily they scoff the bread,
Swallowed down with all the thread.

When they're finished, they discover
There's no escape from one another!

Strung together, tied up hard—
Panic spreads throughout the yard...

All aflutter, in despair,
See them fly up in the air!

See them caught up on the tree,
Squawking out so desperately.
Hear their cries grow strong and stronger,
As their necks stretch long and longer...

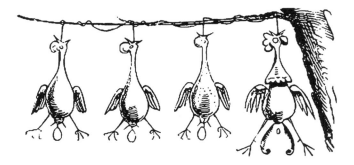

Each chick lays just one last egg,
Then falls lifeless, noiseless, dead.

Widow Palmer, as you see,
Wakes to this cacophony.

Wracked with dread and filled with fright,
She stumbles on the grisly sight.

Soon she's lost to bitter tears:
"All my hope for future years,
All I had to live upon,
Hangs before me—dead and gone!"
Deeply shaken, this good wife
Reaches for her kitchen knife;

Cuts the chickens from the bough,
And wonders what she can do now.

Grey and silent as a mouse,
She trudges back inside the house.

And so the first mean prank is done,
But watch out—here's a second one!

Second Prank

Though still reeling from the shock,
Widow Palmer soon took stock.
Turned things over in her mind,
To see what comfort she could find.
What last tribute could she pay
To such dear creatures snatched away?
Eventually, she formed a plan
To stick them in the frying pan.
But, still, it was a sorry sight,
To see them laid out, pale and white,
Plucked and waiting on the stove,
These four birds who'd loved to rove
Through the yard, around the farm,
Blissful, carefree, safe from harm.

All alone with her dog Ben,
Widow Palmer sobs again.
Hearing this sad sound of weeping,
Max and Moritz soon come creeping.

When they smell it's dinner time,
On the roof they quickly climb.
Down the chimney they go looking,
Spot the chickens gently cooking.

Widow Palmer, unawares,
Heads off down the cellar stairs—

One thing she can't live without
Is her homemade sauerkraut.
What a feast it's bound to make,
Warmed up with her chicken bake!

But she cannot guess the truth
Of what is happ'ning on her roof.
Planning well ahead of time,
Max has brought his fishing line...

In a flash the cheeky crook
Has snared the first bird on his hook.
Shortly after, number two,
Then the third is lifted too.
The rooster flies up last of all,
And Max and Moritz have their haul!
Ben the dog, who sees all this,
Barks and barks to warn his miss.

But it comes too late to matter:
The boys have scarpered down the ladder.

Huffing up the other way,
What will Widow Palmer say?
See her rooted to the spot,
As she spies the empty pot.

When she screams her poor dog's name,
It's obvious who will get the blame.

"Ben!" she squawks, "You filthy sinner!
I'll teach you not to eat my dinner!"

Swinging wildly with her spoon,
She chases him around the room.
Hear him yelping loud and long,
This poor young pup who's done no wrong!

Snoring soundly in the hay,
Max and Moritz hide away.
Of their mean and nasty theft,
A chicken leg is all that's left.

And so the second prank is done,
But watch out—here's another one!

Third Prank

Every village-dweller knows
Of the man who fixes clothes.

Casual dresses, Sunday best,
Trousers, waistcoats, pants or vest,
Fur-trimmed coats and three-piece suits,
Slippers, moccasins and boots,
Silken scarf or threadbare sock,
Take them all to Mister Bock.

Any item for repair,
He'll accept with loving care.
Small jobs, too, get his heart racing
—even buttons, for replacing.
Taking up or letting down,
Back or front or all around,
Working clothes or heights of fashion,
Mending them is Bock's life's passion.
A master of the thread and needle,
He's loved by all the village people.
But Max and Moritz had a plan
To ridicule this gentle man.

Just outside old Bock's front door,
See the fast, cold river roar.

A plank leads to the other side,
'Tis three feet long and two feet wide.

Full of cunning like before,
Max comes running with a saw.
On the bridge he soon sets to it—
Quickly saws a crack half through it.

Once they're done, these nasty boys,
Start to make a hideous noise:

"Tailor Bock, you weird old man,
Na, na! Catch us—if you can!"
A gentle soul of quite some age,
Bock would seldom suffer rage,
But when he hears this rude refrain,
Something snaps inside his brain.

Leaping 'cross his doorstep quick,
Bock comes running with his stick.
Twelve more steps, eleven, ten...
"Na, na, na!" they call again.

Suddenly a giant crack—
As tailor Bock lands in the trap!

"Na, na, na!" the two boys scream,
As—splash!—he tumbles in the stream!

Max and Moritz run off fast,
But luckily two geese swim past.

Close to drowning, near defeat,
Bock grabs wildly at their feet.

Taking one bird in each hand,
He makes it back to solid land.

Still alive, at any rate,
Bock is feeling far from great...

See him suffer, poor old wretch—
Soaked and frozen, muscles stretched.

Fortunately, Mrs Bock
Has her iron nice and hot.
Presses down with all her might,
Until her husband feels all right.

Now that Bock is on the mend,
Perhaps there'll be a happy end?

But that was just prank number three,
The fourth is coming rapidly!

Fourth Prank

One thing we all know—or ought to—
Is that children must be taught to.
But to climb the social tree
Takes much more than ABC.
Proper folk of proper breeding,
Need to know much more than reading...
Adding up and multiplying
Are just fine—but really trying
To improve your social station
Needs grace and sophistication.
Mister Lampel led the class
In making sure this came to pass.

Max and Moritz, no great shock,
Hate him even more than Bock.
Clearly, two such wicked creatures
Don't have any time for teachers.

Lampel hated luxury,
But did have one vice, as you'll see:
At the setting of the sun,
When his working day was done,
Lampel loved to light his pipe
And puff tobacco through the night.
Max and Moritz, quite obsessed
With shattering the poor man's rest,
Decide to cause a massive fright
The moment that his pipe's alight.
One dark Sunday, evening-time,
They embark upon their crime...

While old Lampel's on his perch,
Playing organ in the church,
Max and Moritz quietly glide
Up to his house and sneak inside.

It doesn't take them long at all
To spot his pipe against the wall.

Keen to make our story louder,
Moritz fills it with gunpowder;
Urged on by an evil motive,
He's made Lampel's pipe explosive!
Suddenly Max gives a shout:
"Hurry up! He's coming out!"

Luckily they're not too late—
Lampel has to lock the gate.

Music tucked under his arm,
See this man of grace and charm...

...heading home without a care,
Without a clue who's just been there!

Desperate now to rest his feet,
Lampel lights his smoky treat.

"Ahh," he sighs, "There's nothing ever
Pleases more than simple pleasure!"

BOOM! Those two malicious twits
Succeed in blowing "Sir" to bits!

Coffee pot and jar and kettle,
Shattered glass and twisted metal.
Oven, table, comfy chair—
All gets blasted in the air.

Slowly, as the black smoke clears,
A chargrilled figure now appears.
Surely, Lampel must be charmed—
He's still alive! (Though not unharmed.)

Ear to ear and head to foot,
His skin is scorched, as black as soot.
Where his hair hung, long and full,
There's nothing left but smouldering skull.

Who will teach the children now,
Show them how to scrape and bow?
"And," the village council asks,
"Who'll perform all Lampel's tasks?"
And how is Lampel going to smoke,
Now his precious pipe is broke?

Time heals all, or so they say.
(The pipe might not quite feel that way.)

And so we're done with mean prank four,
But rest assured, there's plenty more!

Fifth Prank

It's not always easy, is it,
When your grandpa comes to visit?
If he is the grumpy type
You will have to be polite.
Say "Good morning!" nice and clear,
Tell him what he wants to hear,
Bring him all the stuff he needs,
Lighter, pipe and things to read.
Or perhaps his back is sore?
Needing rubbing, nothing more?
You'll of course do anything
To ease your grandpa's suffering.
If he's had a sneezing fit,
That's shaken him a little bit,
You'll say, "Bless you, Grandpa dear,"
And hold his hand to soothe his fear.

If he comes round yours to stay,
You'll help him fold his clothes away,
Fetch a nightcap for his head,
Put warm blankets on his bed.
Basically, do all you can
To take care of this poor old man.

Max and Moritz, as you'll see,
Saw things slightly differently...
Grandpa Fritz (a frail old guy)
Would be such fun to terrify!

This was at the time of year
When May bugs start to reappear,
Buzzing round in all the trees,
Biting, scratching all they please.

Max and Moritz, full of glee,
Shake the bugs down from the tree.

Cackling Moritz, giggling Max,
Wrap them up in paper bags;

Take the nasty little "treats"
And stuff them in their grandpa's sheets!

Pulling on his sleeping cap,
Fritz is ready for a nap.

Eyes clamped shut and breathing deep,
Soon enough he's fast asleep.

Snick-snick-snack... The insect horde
Come looking for some flesh to gorge!

Soon the leading May bug goes
And grabs hold of the old man's nose.

"Argh!" Fritz wakes in shock and fear,
And pulls a May bug from his ear.

Nightmare visions in his head,
Grandpa Fritz leaps out of bed.

"Ouch!" A bite, and yet one more,
As Grandpa Fritz skips round the floor!

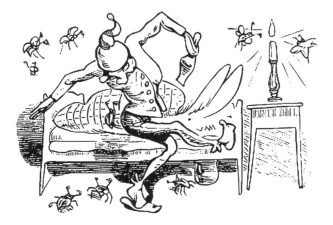

All around, each way he turns,
It itches, scratches, bites and burns.

Barely stopping to draw breath,
He splats and crunches them to death.

His work is finally complete
When all lie squished beneath his feet.

One huge yawn, three big sighs,
And Grandpa Fritz can close his eyes.

And so the fifth mean prank is done,
But watch out—here's another one!

Sixth Prank

Easter is a time of year
That children celebrate with cheer.
In the air there's no mistaking
Smells of sweet things gently baking—
Treats for children who've been nice,
But Max and Moritz want their slice!

Having been caught out before,
The baker carefully locks his door.

But Max and Moritz won't be stopped.
They know that chimneys can't be locked!

Whoosh! Like two great lumps of coal,
They fly, soot-blackened, down the hole...

Whomp! They land with quite some power
In the baker's crate of flour.

Still all smiles, they start to walk,
Both of them now white as chalk.

Spying pretzels on the shelf,
Neither can control himself...

...until the chair breaks into bits...

And plops them in the baker's mix!

Batter dripping from their features,
See them rise like monstrous creatures.

Now the baker comes back home,
And spots the two strange lumps of dough,

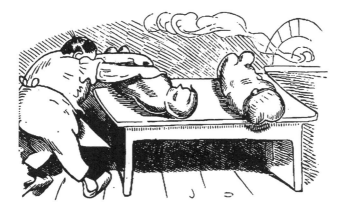

Grabs the helpless, dripping oafs
And rolls them into two huge loaves!

Laid out on the board so neat,
It's time to face the oven's heat.

In they go and out they come,
Brown and crisp and nicely done.

But don't yet mourn these boys-turned-bread,
It turns out that they're not quite dead!

Munch, munch, munch, like little mice,
They eat their way out in a trice.

Shocked, the baker gives a cough:
"Oh, good Lord! My bread's gone off!"

Max and Moritz race off fast,
But this next trick will be their last...

Final Prank

Max and Moritz, can't you see?
This is your last chance to flee!
But somehow they just can't refrain
From slashing holes in sacks of grain.

The farmer comes to take one sack
And lifts it high upon his back.

But as he staggers for the door,
The grain starts falling to the floor.

Hear the poor old baffled blighter:
"What the—? It's getting lighter!"

Two heads poking from the grain
Tell the farmer who's to blame.

With a loud, resounding smack,
He shovels them inside the sack.

Max and Moritz feel quite ill,
As they're carried to the mill.

"Mister Miller, quickly, man!
Grind this up as fast you can!"

Sure enough, he tips each brute
Head first down the metal chute.

Chop, chop, chop, chop, chop, chop, chop...
Once the mill starts, it won't stop!

One last time we see our chums,
Ground down into tiny crumbs...

...till the very last small piece
Is swallowed by the miller's geese!

Conclusion

In the village news spreads fast,
But the sorrow doesn't last...
The widow who first lost her birds
Thinks: "They got what they deserved!"
"Evil doesn't pay," nods Bock,
Smiling as he darns a sock.
In the schoolhouse, Mister Lampel
Says: "It's just one more example..."
But the baker's not so hasty,
Points out that "They were quite tasty..."
Even Grandpa Fritz agrees
That boys can't just do as they please.
The farmer, somewhat sheepishly,
Says: "What's it got to do with me?"
So, in short, without those boys,
All the village can rejoice.
"Thank the Lord! We can relax,
Goodbye Moritz, Goodbye Max!"

Max und Moritz

(Original German Text)

Ach, was muß man oft von bösen
Kindern hören oder lesen!
Wie zum Beispiel hier von diesen,
Welche Max und Moritz hießen.
Die, anstatt durch weise Lehren
Sich zum Guten zu bekehren,
Oftmals noch darüber lachten
Und sich heimlich lustig machten.—
—Ja, zur Übeltätigkeit,
Ja, dazu ist man bereit!—
—Menschen necken, Tiere quälen,
Äpfel, Birnen, Zwetschgen stehlen—
Das ist freilich angenehmer
Und dazu auch viel bequemer,
Als in Kirche oder Schule

Festzusitzen auf dem Stuhle.—
Aber wehe, wehe, wehe!
Wenn ich auf das Ende sehe!!—
Ach, das war ein schlimmes Ding,
Wie es Max und Moritz ging.
—Drum ist hier, was sie getrieben,
Abgemalt und aufgeschrieben.
Mancher gibt sich viele Müh'
Mit dem lieben Federvieh;
Einesteils der Eier wegen,
Welche diese Vögel legen,
Zweitens: Weil man dann und wann
Einen Braten essen kann;
Drittens aber nimmt man auch
Ihre Federn zum Gebrauch
In die Kissen und die Pfühle,
Denn man liegt nicht gerne kühle.—
Seht, da ist die Witwe Bolte,
Die das auch nicht gerne wollte.
Ihrer Hühner waren drei
Und ein stolzer Hahn dabei.—
Max und Moritz dachten nun:
Was ist hier jetzt wohl zu tun?—
Ganz geschwinde, eins, zwei, drei
Schneiden sie sich Brot entzwei,

In vier Teile jedes Stück
Wie ein kleiner Finger dick.
Diese binden sie an Fäden,
Übers Kreuz, ein Stück an jeden,
Und verlegen sie genau
In den Hof der guten Frau.—
Kaum hat dies der Hahn gesehen,
Fängt er auch schon an zu krähen:
Kikeriki! Kikikerikih!!
Tak, tak, tak!—da kommen sie.
Hahn und Hühner schlucken munter
Jedes ein Stück Brot hinunter;
Aber als sie sich besinnen,
Konnte keines recht von hinnen.
In die Kreuz und in die Quer
Reißen sie sich hin und her,
Flattern auf und in die Höh',
Ach herje, herjemineh!
Ach, sie bleiben an dem langen,
Dürren Ast des Baumes hangen.—
Und ihr Hals wird lang und länger,
Ihr Gesang wird bang und bänger.
Jedes legt noch schnell ein Ei,
Und dann kommt der Tod herbei.—
Witwe Bolte in der Kammer

Hört im Bette diesen Jammer:
Ahnungsvoll tritt sie heraus,
Ach, was war das für ein Graus!
"Fließet aus dem Aug', ihr Tränen!
All' mein Hoffen, all' mein Sehnen,
Meines Lebens schönster Traum
Hängt an diesem Apfelbaum!"
Tiefbetrübt und sorgenschwer
Kriegt sie jetzt das Messer her,
Nimmt die Toten von den Strängen,
Daß sie so nicht länger hängen,
Und mit stummem Trauerblick
Kehrt sie in ihr Haus zurück.
Dieses war der erste Streich,
Doch der zweite folgt sogleich.
Als die gute Witwe Bolte
Sich von ihrem Schmerz erholte,
Dachte sie so hin und her,
Daß es wohl das beste wär',
Die Verstorb'nen, die hienieden
Schon so frühe abgeschieden,
Ganz im stillen und in Ehren
Gut gebraten zu verzehren.—
Freilich war die Trauer groß,
Als sie nun so nackt und bloß

Abgerupft am Herde lagen,
Sie, die einst in schönen Tagen
Bald im Hofe, bald im Garten
Lebensfroh im Sande scharrten.—
Ach, Frau Bolte weint aufs neu,
Und der Spitz steht auch dabei.
Max und Moritz rochen dieses;
"Schnell aufs Dach gekrochen!" hieß es.
Durch den Schornstein mit Vergnügen
Sehen sie die Hühner liegen,
Die schon ohne Kopf und Gurgeln
Lieblich in der Pfanne schmurgeln.—
Eben geht mit einem Teller
Witwe Bolte in den Keller,
Daß sie von dem Sauerkohle
Eine Portion sich hole,
Wofür sie besonders schwärmt,
Wenn er wieder aufgewärmt.—
Unterdessen auf dem Dache
Ist man tätig bei der Sache.
Max hat schon mit Vorbedacht
Eine Angel mitgebracht.
Schnupdiwup! da wird nach oben
Schon ein Huhn heraufgehoben;
Schnupdiwup! Jetzt Numro zwei;

Schnupdiwup! Jetzt Numro drei;
Und jetzt kommt noch Numro vier:
Schnupdiwup! Dich haben wir!—
Zwar der Spitz sah es genau,
Und er bellt: Rawau! Rawau!
Aber schon sind sie ganz munter
Fort und von dem Dach herunter.—
Na! Das wird Spektakel geben,
Denn Frau Bolte kommt soeben;—
Angewurzelt stand sie da,
Als sie nach der Pfanne sah.
Alle Hühner waren fort,
"Spitz!"—Das war ihr erstes Wort.
"Oh, du Spitz, du Ungetüm!
Aber wart! ich komme ihm!"
Mit dem Löffel, groß und schwer,
Geht es über Spitzen her;
Laut ertönt sein Wehgeschrei,
Denn er fühlt sich schuldenfrei.
Max und Moritz im Verstecke
Schnarchen aber an der Hecke,
Und vom ganzen Hühnerschmaus
Guckt nur noch ein Bein heraus.
Dieses war der zweite Streich,
Doch der dritte folgt sogleich.

Jedermann im Dorfe kannte
Einen, der sich Böck benannte.
Alltagsröcke, Sonntagsröcke,
Lange Hosen, spitze Fräcke,
Westen mit bequemen Taschen,
Warme Mäntel und Gamaschen—
Alle diese Kleidungssachen
Wußte Schneider Böck zu machen.—
Oder wäre was zu flicken,
Abzuschneiden, anzustücken,
Oder gar ein Knopf der Hose
Abgerissen oder lose—
Wie und wo und wann es sei,
Hinten, vorne, einerlei—
Alles macht der Meister Böck,
Denn das ist sein Lebenszweck.
D'rum so hat in der Gemeinde
Jedermann ihn gern zum Freunde.—
Aber Max und Moritz dachten,
Wie sie ihn verdrießlich machten.
Nämlich vor des Meisters Hause
Floß ein Wasser mit Gebrause.
Übers Wasser führt ein Steg
Und darüber geht der Weg.
Max und Moritz, gar nicht träge,

Sägen heimlich mit der Säge,
Ritzeratze! voller Tücke,
In die Brücke eine Lücke.
Als nun diese Tat vorbei,
Hört man plötzlich ein Geschrei:
"He, heraus! du Ziegen-Böck!
Schneider, Schneider, meck, meck, meck!"—
Alles konnte Böck ertragen,
Ohne nur ein Wort zu sagen;
Aber, wenn er dies erfuhr,
Ging's ihm wider die Natur.
Schnelle springt er mit der Elle
Über seines Hauses Schwelle,
Denn schon wieder ihm zum Schreck
Tönt ein lautes: "Meck, meck, meck!"
Und schon ist er auf der Brücke,
Kracks! Die Brücke bricht in Stücke;
Wieder tönt es: "Meck, meck, meck!"
Plumps! Da ist der Schneider weg!
G'rad als dieses vorgekommen,
Kommt ein Gänsepaar geschwommen,
Welches Böck in Todeshast
Krampfhaft bei den Beinen faßt.
Beide Gänse in der Hand,
Flattert er auf trocknes Land.

Übrigens bei alle dem
Ist so etwas nicht bequem!
Wie denn Böck von der Geschichte
Auch das Magendrücken kriegte.
Hoch ist hier Frau Böck zu preisen!
Denn ein heißes Bügeleisen,
Auf den kalten Leib gebracht,
Hat es wieder gut gemacht.
Bald im Dorf hinauf, hinunter,
Hieß es, Böck ist wieder munter.
Dieses war der dritte Streich,
Doch der vierte folgt sogleich.
Also lautet ein Beschluß:
Daß der Mensch was lernen muß.—
Nicht allein das Abc
Bringt den Menschen in die Höh';
Nicht allein im Schreiben, Lesen
Übt sich ein vernünftig Wesen;
Nicht allein in Rechnungssachen
Soll der Mensch sich Mühe machen;
Sondern auch der Weisheit Lehren
Muß man mit Vergnügen hören.
Daß dies mit Verstand geschah,
War Herr Lehrer Lämpel da.—
Max und Moritz, diese beiden,

Mochten ihn darum nicht leiden;
Denn wer böse Streiche macht,
Gibt nicht auf den Lehrer acht.
Nun war dieser brave Lehrer
Von dem Tobak ein Verehrer,
Was man ohne alle Frage
Nach des Tages Müh und Plage
Einem guten, alten Mann
Auch von Herzen gönnen kann.—
Max und Moritz, unverdrossen,
Sinnen aber schon auf Possen,
Ob vermittelst seiner Pfeifen
Dieser Mann nicht anzugreifen.—
Einstens, als es Sonntag wieder
Und Herr Lämpel brav und bieder
In der Kirche mit Gefühle
Saß vor seinem Orgelspiele,
Schlichen sich die bösen Buben
In sein Haus und seine Stuben,
Wo die Meerschaumpfeife stand;
Max hält sie in seiner Hand;
Aber Moritz aus der Tasche
Zieht die Flintenpulverflasche,
Und geschwinde, stopf, stopf, stopf!
Pulver in den Pfeifenkopf.—

Jetzt nur still und schnell nach Haus,
Denn schon ist die Kirche aus.—
Eben schließt in sanfter Ruh'
Lämpel seine Kirche zu;
Und mit Buch und Notenheften,
Nach besorgten Amtsgeschäften,
Lenkt er freudig seine Schritte
Zu der heimatlichen Hütte,
Und voll Dankbarkeit sodann,
Zündet er sein Pfeifchen an.
"Ach!"—spricht er—"die größte Freud'
Ist doch die Zufriedenheit!"
Rums! Da geht die Pfeife los
Mit Getöse, schrecklich groß.
Kaffeetopf und Wasserglas,
Tabaksdose, Tintenfaß,
Ofen, Tisch und Sorgensitz—
Alles fliegt im Pulverblitz.
Als der Dampf sich nun erhob,
Sieht man Lämpel, der—gottlob!—
Lebend auf dem Rücken liegt;
Doch er hat was abgekriegt.
Nase, Hand, Gesicht und Ohren
Sind so schwarz als wie die Mohren,
Und des Haares letzter Schopf

Ist verbrannt bis auf den Kopf.
Wer soll nun die Kinder lehren
Und die Wissenschaft vermehren?
Wer soll nun für Lämpel leiten
Seine Amtestätigkeiten?
Woraus soll der Lehrer rauchen,
Wenn die Pfeife nicht zu brauchen?
Mit der Zeit wird alles heil,
Nur die Pfeife hat ihr Teil.
Dieses war der vierte Streich,
Doch der fünfte folgt sogleich.
Wer im Dorfe oder Stadt
Einen Onkel wohnen hat,
Der sei höflich und bescheiden,
Denn das mag der Onkel leiden.—
Morgens sagt man: "Guten Morgen!
Haben Sie was zu besorgen?"
Bringt ihm, was er haben muß:
Zeitung, Pfeife, Fidibus.—
Oder sollt' es wo im Rücken
Drücken, beißen oder zwicken,
Gleich ist man mit Freudigkeit
Dienstbeflissen und bereit.—
Oder sei's nach einer Prise,
Daß der Onkel heftig niese,

Ruft man: "Prosit!" allsogleich,
"Danke, wohl bekomm' es euch!"—
Oder kommt er spät nach Haus,
Zieht man ihm die Stiefel aus,
Holt Pantoffel, Schlafrock, Mütze,
Daß er nicht im Kalten sitze,—
Kurz, man ist darauf bedacht,
Was dem Onkel Freude macht.—
Max und Moritz ihrerseits
Fanden darin keinen Reiz.—
Denkt euch nur, welch' schlechten Witz
Machten sie mit Onkel Fritz!
Jeder weiß, was so ein Mai—
Käfer für ein Vogel sei.
In den Bäumen hin und her
Fliegt und kriecht und krabbelt er.
Max und Moritz, immer munter,
Schütteln sie vom Baum herunter.
In die Düte von Papiere
Sperren sie die Krabbeltiere.
Fort damit und in die Ecke
Unter Onkel Fritzens Decke!
Bald zu Bett geht Onkel Fritze
In der spitzen Zippelmütze;
Seine Augen macht er zu,

Hüllt sich ein und schläft in Ruh.
Doch die Käfer, kritze, kratze!
Kommen schnell aus der Matratze.
Schon faßt einer, der voran,
Onkel Fritzens Nase an.
"Bau!" schreit er—"Was ist das hier?"
Und erfaßt das Ungetier.
Und den Onkel voller Grausen
Sieht man aus dem Bette sausen.
"Autsch!"—Schon wieder hat er einen
Im Genicke, an den Beinen;
Hin und her und rund herum
Kriecht es, fliegt es mit Gebrumm.
Onkel Fritz, in dieser Not,
Haut und trampelt alles tot.
Guckste wohl! Jetzt ist's vorbei
Mit der Käferkrabbelei!
Onkel Fritz hat wieder Ruh'
Und macht seine Augen zu.
Dieses war der fünfte Streich,
Doch der sechste folgt sogleich.
In der schönen Osterzeit,
Wenn die frommen Bäckersleut'
Viele süße Zuckersachen
Backen und zurechte machen,

Wünschten Max und Moritz auch
Sich so etwas zum Gebrauch.
Doch der Bäcker, mit Bedacht,
Hat das Backhaus zugemacht.
Also will hier einer stehlen,
Muß er durch den Schlot sich quälen.
Ratsch! Da kommen die zwei Knaben
Durch den Schornstein, schwarz wie Raben.
Puff! Sie fallen in die Kist',
Wo das Mehl darinnen ist.
Da! Nun sind sie alle beide,
Rund herum so weiß wie Kreide.
Aber schon mit viel Vergnügen
Sehen sie die Brezeln liegen.
Knacks!—Da bricht der Stuhl entzwei;
Schwapp!—Da liegen sie im Brei.
Ganz von Kuchenteig umhüllt,
Steh'n sie da als Jammerbild.—
Gleich erscheint der Meister Bäcker
Und bemerkt die Zuckerlecker.
Eins, zwei, drei!—eh' man's gedacht,
Sind zwei Brote d'raus gemacht.
In dem Ofen glüht es noch—
Ruff!—damit ins Ofenloch!
Ruff!—man zieht sie aus der Glut;

Denn nun sind sie braun und gut.—
Jeder denkt, die sind perdü!
Aber nein—noch leben sie.
Knusper, Knasper!—wie zwei Mäuse
Fressen sie durch das Gehäuse;
Und der Meister Bäcker schrie:
"Ach herrjeh! da laufen sie!"
Dieses war der sechste Streich,
Doch der letzte folgt sogleich.
Max und Moritz, wehe euch!
Jetzt kommt euer letzter Streich!
Wozu müssen auch die beiden
Löcher in die Säcke schneiden?
Seht, da trägt der Bauer Mecke
Einen seiner Maltersäcke.
Aber kaum, daß er von hinnen,
Fängt das Korn schon an zu rinnen.
Und verwundert steht und spricht er:
"Zapperment! dat Ding werd lichter!"
Hei! Da sieht er voller Freude
Max und Moritz im Getreide.
Rabs!—in seinen großen Sack
Schaufelt er das Lumpenpack.
Max und Moritz wird es schwüle,
Denn nun geht es nach der Mühle.—

"Meister Müller, he, heran!
Mahl er das, so schnell er kann!"
"Her damit!" Und in den Trichter
Schüttelt er die Bösewichter.—
Rickeracke! Rickeracke!
Geht die Mühle mit Geknacke.
Hier kann man sie noch erblicken
Fein geschroten und in Stücken.
Doch sogleich verzehret sie
Meister Müllers Federvieh.
Als man dies im Dorf erfuhr,
War von Trauer keine Spur.—
Witwe Bolte, mild und weich,
Sprach: "Sieh' da, ich dacht' es gleich!"—
"Ja, ja, ja!" rief Meister Böck,
"Bosheit ist kein Lebenszweck!"—
Drauf so sprach Herr Lehrer Lämpel:
"Dies ist wieder ein Exempel!"—
"Freilich!" meint der Zuckerbäcker,
"Warum ist der Mensch so lecker!"—
Selbst der gute Onkel Fritze
Sprach: "Das kommt von dumme Witze!"—
Doch der brave Bauersmann
Dachte: "Wat geiht meck dat an!"—
Kurz im ganzen Ort herum

Ging ein freudiges Gebrumm:
"Gott sei Dank! Nun ist's vorbei
Mit der Übeltäterei!!"

Translator's Note

First published in 1865, the same year in which Lewis Carroll produced *Alice's Adventures in Wonderland*, Wilhelm Busch's *Max und Moritz* needs little introduction to German-speaking readers. The mock cautionary tale of two young boys who terrorize the bourgeois inhabitants of their village, before coming to a sticky end themselves, brought the 33-year-old illustrator and poet almost instant fame. By the time of Busch's death in 1908, the tale had gone through fifty-six editions and sold more than 430,000 copies. By 1925, sixty years after its original publication, *Max und Moritz* had reached its hundredth edition and racked up more than 1.5 million sales. Today, it remains a classic of German children's literature, with its author frequently hailed in his homeland as one of the forefathers of modern comic books.

Despite dozens of translations and adaptations, *Max und Moritz* has not enjoyed anywhere near as much popularity in the English-speaking world. I believe that this is in no small part down to the nature of many of those previous translations, which have tended to follow the precise wording of the German too slavishly—at the expense of the linguistic "flow" found within Busch's original text. Maintaining the rhyming couplet structure of the tale while translating the words into another language is certainly not a simple task, but in this new translation (published a little more than 150 years after the original) I have attempted a slightly looser style, seeking to convey the fun and energy of the German original without, hopefully, straying too far from the source.

Often this has only been made possible by slight alterations to the ordering of sentence parts, or by placing a greater emphasis on the general gist of what Busch wrote, rather than literally translating every word and phrase. On very few occasions, I have made changes to the text in order to make it more readily understandable to a modern audience, and particularly to younger readers who are unlikely to be familiar with words such as "spats", "inkpots" or references to elderly relatives sneezing heavily after taking large pinches of snuff!

I have also taken the liberty of changing some of the characters' names, with Witwe Bolte now turned into Widow Palmer ("A kind and gentle lady farmer") while Lämpel and

Böck both lose the umlauts from their surnames. After some deliberation, I have also "aged" "Onkel Fritz" into "Grandpa Fritz", reasoning that uncles are no longer seen by today's children as the elderly, authoritarian figures that they may have been perceived as in Busch's time—although that may just be wishful thinking, now that I am an uncle myself!

For those who speak both German and English (or are perhaps learning one of the languages), the original German version has been included immediately after the English translation—and I hope that this will provide added value, by allowing readers to spot where I have made tweaks to improve the flow of the English translation.

The only phrase that I have deliberately altered due to its being significantly out of step with modern sensitivities comes in the section after Herr Lampel, the boys' sanctimonious teacher, has narrowly escaped being blown apart by the gunpowder which they had stuffed into his pipe. "Nase, Hand, Gesicht und Ohren / Sind so schwarz als wie die Mohren" ("Nose, hand, face and ears / Are as black as those of the Moors") has an obvious literary resonance with Othello, but otherwise seems an unnecessarily outdated phrase to keep in. Instead, I have opted for a less jarring "Ear to ear and head to foot / His skin is scorched, as black as soot".

Given its dark tones, some will perhaps question whether *Max and Moritz* is even a children's book. Busch himself appears to have intended the work for an older audience—submitting the tale to the publisher Kaspar Braun in the belief that it would appear in the satirical weekly newspaper *Fliegende Blätter*. It was Braun who made the decision (subsequently vindicated) to publish the story via his children's book division. Still, questions about the tale's suitability for children continued to be raised by Busch's contemporaries. In 1883, the critic Friedrich Seidel launched a scathing attack, claiming that "these caricatures... in *Max and Moritz* and other works by W. Busch, which at first glance seem so harmless and humorous, are one of the extremely dangerous poisons that are turning the youth of today... into such frivolous, insubordinate know-it-alls".

It is true that there are no simple moral lessons to be found in *Max and Moritz*—in stark contrast to the ploddingly didactic cautionary tales which Busch and other nineteenth-century humorists (such as the *Struwwelpeter* author Heinrich Hoffmann) were clearly parodying. The individual pranks, meanwhile, are barely distinguishable from wanton acts of violence, theft and destruction, which go far beyond mere naughtiness or mischief.

Further complicating the sense of "right" and "wrong" in the story, none of the "victims" are portrayed in a particularly positive light, especially at the end, when they are all shown to have been, to a varying extent, complicit in the grisly demise of the two boys. One appraisal of the story's subtext, published a few years ago on the German language website The German Professor, went so far as to suggest that Busch "exposes the coldness and harshness of an authoritarian society and unmasks the moral hypocrisy inherent in the violent removal of those who violate [its] sense of order".

Serious stuff! But while there is certainly plenty in *Max and Moritz* for adult readers to sink their teeth into, it can surely also be read and enjoyed by all but the most squeamish of youngsters. The comic-book nature of the boys' crimes, as depicted by Busch, ensures that they are unlikely to shock modern children (and their parents) who have grown up with the darkly humorous tales of recent children's literature, perhaps most prominently the hugely successful works of Roald Dahl. While translating *Max und Moritz*, I did wonder whether the act of stuffing gunpowder into a teacher's pipe in an attempt to blow him up might be considered a bit excessive for modern readers—only to come across an almost identical scenario carried out by the sympathetic heroine of David Walliams's 2014 book *Awful Auntie*.

It is arguably the first prank of all that might cause the most offence today, involving as it does the killing of four defenceless farm birds. Quite why cruelty to animals should appear worse to modern readers than cruelty to people (at least in terms of cartoon violence) is probably too big an issue to address properly here, but parents of young, animal-loving children should almost certainly read through the first prank at the very least, before deciding whether they wish to add *Max and Moritz* to their stack of bedtime reading!

That (slight) warning aside, whether you are nine or ninety-nine, a total newcomer to the story or someone who is familiar with the German original but yet to find a good English rendition—I hope you enjoy this new translation of the misadventures of two young boys, who are still looking surprisingly sprightly as they celebrate more than 150 years of mischief-making!

MARK LEDSOM
Olney, April 2019

PUSHKIN CHILDREN'S BOOKS

We created Pushkin Children's Books to share tales from different languages and cultures with younger readers, and to open the door to the wide, colourful worlds these stories offer.

From picture books and adventure stories to fairy tales and classics, and from fifty-year-old bestsellers to current huge successes abroad, the books on the Pushkin Children's list reflect the very best stories from around the world, for our most discerning readers of all: children.

THE BEGINNING WOODS
MALCOLM MCNEILL

'I loved every word and was envious of quite a few... A modern classic. Rich, funny and terrifying'
Eoin Colfer

THE RED ABBEY CHRONICLES
MARIA TURTSCHANINOFF

1 · *Maresi*
2 · *Naondel*

'Embued with myth, wonder, and told with a dazzling, compelling ferocity'
Kiran Millwood Hargrave, author of *The Girl of Ink and Stars*

THE LETTER FOR THE KING
TONKE DRAGT

'*The Letter for the King* will get pulses racing... Pushkin Press deserves every praise for publishing this beautifully translated, well-presented and captivating book'
The Times

THE SECRETS OF THE WILD WOOD
TONKE DRAGT

'Offers intrigue, action and escapism'
Sunday Times

THE SONG OF SEVEN
TONKE DRAGT

'A cracking adventure... so nail-biting you'll need to wear protective gloves'
The Times

THE MURDERER'S APE
JAKOB WEGELIUS

'A thrilling adventure. Prepare to meet the remarkable Sally Jones; you won't soon forget her'
Publishers Weekly

THE PARENT TRAP · THE FLYING CLASSROOM · DOT AND ANTON

ERICH KÄSTNER

Illustrated by Walter Trier

'The bold line drawings by Walter Trier are the work of genius... As for the stories, if you're a fan of *Emil and the Detectives*, then you'll find these just as spirited'

Spectator

FROM THE MIXED-UP FILES OF MRS. BASIL E. FRANKWEILER

E. L. KONIGSBURG

'Delightful... I love this book... a beautifully written adventure, with endearing characters and full of dry wit, imagination and inspirational confidence'

Daily Mail

THE RECKLESS SERIES

CORNELIA FUNKE

1 · *The Petrified Flesh*
2 · *Living Shadows*
3 · *The Golden Yarn*

'A wonderful storyteller'

Sunday Times

THE WILDWITCH SERIES

LENE KAABERBØL

1 · *Wildfire*
2 · *Oblivion*
3 · *Life Stealer*
4 · *Bloodling*

'Classic fantasy adventure... Young readers will be delighted to hear that there are more adventures to come for Clara'

Lovereading

MEET AT THE ARK AT EIGHT!

ULRICH HUB

Illustrated by Jörg Mühle

'Of all the books about a penguin in a suitcase pretending to be God asking for a cheesecake, this one is absolutely, definitely my favourite'

Independent

THE SNOW QUEEN

HANS CHRISTIAN ANDERSEN

Illustrated by Lucie Arnoux

'A lovely edition [of a] timeless story'

The Lady

THE WILD SWANS

HANS CHRISTIAN ANDERSEN

'A fresh new translation of these two classic fairy tales recreates the lyrical beauty and pathos of the Danish genius' evergreen stories'

The Bay

THE CAT WHO CAME IN OFF THE ROOF

ANNIE M.G. SCHMIDT

'Guaranteed to make anyone 7-plus to 107 who likes to curl up with a book and a cat purr with pleasure'

The Times

LAFCADIO: THE LION WHO SHOT BACK

SHEL SILVERSTEIN

'A story which is really funny, yet also teaches us a great deal about what we want, what we think we want and what we are no longer certain about once we have it'

Irish Times

THE SECRET OF THE BLUE GLASS

TOMIKO INUI

'I love this book... How important it is, in these times, that our children read the stories from other peoples, other cultures, other times'

Michael Morpurgo, *Guardian*

THE STORY OF THE BLUE PLANET

ANDRI SNÆR MAGNASON

Illustrated by Áslaug Jónsdóttir

'A Seussian mix of wonder, wit and gravitas'

The New York Times